Diary of a
Monster's Son

Diary of a Monster's Son

by **Ellen Conford**

Illustrated by
Tom Newsom

SCHOLASTIC INC.
New York Toronto London Auckland Sydney
Mexico City New Delhi Hong Kong Buenos Aires

For David,
who has monstrously good ideas
— E.C.

Text copyright © 1999 by Ellen Conford.
Illustrations copyright © 1999 by Tom Newsom.
All rights reserved. Published by Scholastic Inc.,
557 Broadway, New York, NY 10012,
by arrangement with Little, Brown and Company (Inc.)
Printed in the U.S.A.

ISBN 0-439-58177-X

1 2 3 4 5 6 7 8 9 10   40   12 11 10 09 08 07 06 05 04 03

"Clothes Make the Monster"

August 28

When I wake up this morning, I hear my father whistling in the bathroom.

The door is open, so I go in.

He is standing in front of the mirror, combing his hair.

"Good morning, Bradley," he says. "Isn't this a beautiful day?"

I wish I had hair like my father's. It's long and dark and thick. My hair is short and light and stubby. It is only on my head.

I watch as he brushes his teeth. My father has outstanding teeth. They are big and pointy and white. The two on the sides come way down over his bottom lip.

He is very proud of them. He polishes them

three times a day and sees the dentist twice a year.

"Take care of your fangs," he always says, "and your fangs will take care of you."

"But I don't have fangs," I tell him. "I just have plain little tiny teeth."

"Proper dental care is important," he tells me. "Even for little tiny teeth."

When he is finished in the bathroom, I brush my little tiny teeth. Then I get dressed and go down to the kitchen.

My father is mixing something in a big bowl. "Would you like waffles today?" he asks.

"Yes!" I would always like waffles.

He gets out the waffle iron and puts it on the counter. Then he looks at me in surprise.

"Bradley, when did you get so big?"

I look down at myself. "Am I big?"

"You must have grown two inches this summer. Look how short your jeans are."

He stands me next to the back door. He draws a pencil line on the wall.

"See?" he says.

The line is way above the one from last year.

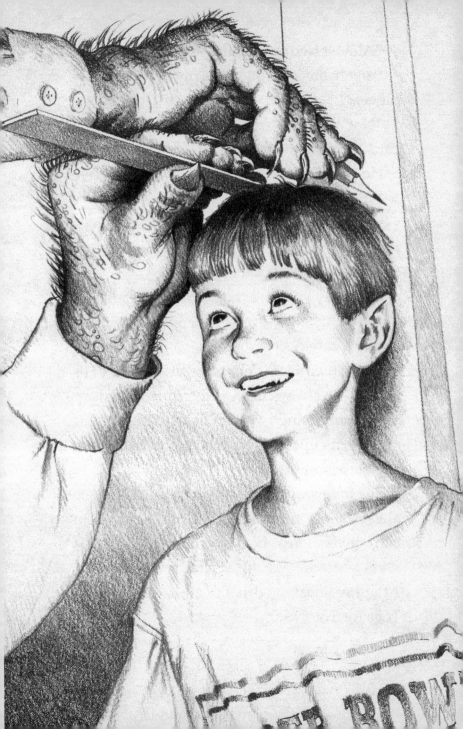

"Almost two and a half inches."

I open my mouth. "Did my teeth get any bigger?"

"Not yet," he says. "But I'm sure they'll catch up with the rest of you."

He plugs in the waffle iron. "We will have to buy you new school clothes."

"Shopping?" I make a face. "Yuck." I hate trying on clothes. "I can still fit into my old stuff."

"The way you dress is important, Bradley. If you're a careless dresser, people may think you're a careless person."

My father is a very careful dresser. His clothes are always fresh and crisply ironed.

The only thing is, when he gets excited, his chest puffs up. It grows bigger and bigger, till sometimes a button from his shirt pops off.

But he always says, "Pardon me." And he always picks up his buttons and sews them back on as soon as he has a chance.

After breakfast we drive to a new store called Togs for Tots.

"I'm not a tot!" I say when I see the store. "Why are we going here?"

He points to a big sign in the window: SUPER BACK-TO-SCHOOL SALE! BIG SAVINGS!!

"But I'm not a tot! And what are togs, anyway?"

" 'Togs' is another word for clothes," he says. He points to another sign on the door: CLOTHES FOR KIDS OF ALL AGES. "See?" he says. "Kids of all ages."

"Then they shouldn't call it Togs for Tots," I say. "I hope I don't see anyone I know in here."

"If you do," he says, "they will be buying clothes, too."

We go inside.

Everybody is buying clothes. The store is bursting. Mothers and fathers and children and salespeople are running around. They grab things off racks and shelves and counters.

Babies are crying. Kids are yelling. There are long lines under the FITTING ROOMS sign. There are long lines at the cash register.

"This place is a zoo!" I say.

"They certainly do look busy," my father agrees.

"I hate buying clothes," I grumble.

"I know." My father puts his hand on my shoulder. "But think of how nice you'll look when we're done."

"We'll never get done," I say.

"Maybe we can find someone to help us." My father pulls a list from his pocket. "Let's see. We need six pairs of pants, eight shirts, socks, and underwear."

"I hate buying underwear," I complain. "Underwear is boring."

"Underwear is important," my father says. "Even if it doesn't show."

We see a salesman. A lady holding a blue dress is tugging at his arm. "Do you have this in a size six?" she asks.

A man with a stroller pushes it right into the salesman's shins. Twin babies are in the stroller. Both babies are screaming. Their faces are bright red.

"Do you have Bunnykins pajamas with

feet?" The man shouts so he can be heard over the screaming.

"I was here first!" the lady holding the blue dress says angrily.

I haven't tried on one piece of clothes yet. And I'm already tired and grumpy.

"This place is full of crazy people," I say. "I don't want new clothes. I want to go home."

"It's not polite to call people crazy," my father says. "The salesman will help us when he has time. We just have to be patient."

But his chest is beginning to puff up. I watch it get bigger and bigger. I can see his buttons straining. I can see bits of hair sticking out between the buttons.

The woman with the blue eyes notices my father. Her eyes grow big. She takes a few steps backward. "I'll look for the dress myself," she says.

She hurries away.

The man with the stroller sees my father.

"Jason and Jessica must be hungry," he says. "I'll come back later." He wheels the stroller around and rushes toward the front of the store.

The salesman turns to face us. His mouth opens wide. But when he talks, his voice is small and squeaky.

"Oh. Goodness."

"My son needs new clothes for school," my father says. "But you look very busy."

"Uh—maybe your son can come back when we're not so busy." The salesman backs away from us. "With his mother."

"I don't have a mother," I say. "Just a father."

"Oh," the salesman says. "I'm sorry."

"It's not your fault," I tell him.

My father hands him our list of clothes.

"We should have everything you need," the salesman says. "Follow me, please." He starts to walk toward the back of the store. Then he turns and looks at us again.

"Excuse me," he says. He holds out his arm. "After *you*."

"There, you see, Bradley?" my father says. "It always pays to be polite."

I try on a gazillion pairs of pants. Jeans, corduroys, khakis. I don't like any of them.

"But they fit well," my father says.

"Very well." The salesman nods.

"They're too skinny," I say. "I like them baggy."

"I don't want you to look sloppy," my father says.

"But everyone wears baggy pants!" I say. "I look stupid in these."

"I think you look very nice," the salesman says.

"I look like a dork."

My father shrugs and smiles at the salesman. His fangs gleam in the fitting-room light. "I guess we'll try on some baggy ones."

"Of course." The salesman runs out of the fitting room. He comes back in a little while with a gazillion more pairs of pants.

I try one on. It looks cool.

"I like these," I say. "I want these." The pants slip down till the elastic on my shorts shows.

"They're too loose," my father says.

"They're perfect," I say.

The pants slide down some more. Now all of my shorts show.

"I might need a belt," I say.

"I told you, Bradley," my father says. "Underwear *is* important."

We make a deal. I can get three pairs of baggy pants. But I have to get three pairs of dorky narrow pants.

My father lets me pick out all the shirts. I let him pick out all the underwear and socks.

Finally we have everything on our list.

The salesman takes us to the cash register. He rings up our order right away. He puts everything in boxes and bags.

"Thank you for shopping at Togs for Tots," he says.

"I'm not a tot," I say.

"Remember your manners, Bradley," my father says.

The salesman pats me on the head. But not

as if he really likes me. It's not that kind of a pat.

"You were very helpful," my father tells him. "We'll be sure to ask for you the next time we're here."

"You don't have to do that," the salesman says quickly. "All our salespeople are very helpful. Any one of them will be glad to take care of you."

The store is much quieter as we leave. The lady with the blue dress is gone. The man with the twins is gone. Some of the salespeople are putting clothes back on the racks. Some are trying to make neat piles of the stuff that got messed up.

We carry our packages out to the car.

"See, Bradley," my father says. "That wasn't so bad."

"It wasn't so good, either," I say. "But it didn't take as long as I thought it would."

"That's because we were polite," my father says. "When you're polite to people, they are happy to help you."

"I don't think that salesman was happy to help me," I say as we drive away.

"I think he must have been very tired." My father smiles. "He did have to deal with a lot of weird people today."

Monster-Teacher Night

September 7

Uh-oh.

Russell Redfern is in my class again.

We have been in the same class since kindergarten. Sometimes he calls me Stinkface. Then I call him Monkey Breath. Then we fight.

Amanda Lake is in my class, too. I like Amanda. She never calls me Stinkface. So we never fight.

I hardly ever fight with anyone. Except Russell.

It is usually his fault.

Mrs. Harper is my teacher this year. She makes me sit next to Russell. I would rather sit next to Amanda.

September 12
....

We have art today. Mr. Vogel is our art teacher. He gives us colored markers and tells us to draw portraits of our desk partners.

I don't want to draw Russell. Russell doesn't want to draw me. We fight over the markers. Russell hogs all the good colors.

Mr. Vogel says we have to share the markers. Russell is not good at sharing.

I start to draw Russell. I make his face round and orange, like a pumpkin. I make his eyes cross, so he looks dopey. I draw red corkscrew squiggles for his hair. But not a lot of corkscrews. Just three, sticking out funny.

I give him green teeth. I draw green stuff coming out of his nose.

When I'm finished, I put down my marker.

"Let me see," Russell says.

I show him my drawing.

"This doesn't look like me!" he yells.

He scrawls a big black X across my portrait.

I reach over and draw a big red X across his nose.

Mr. Vogel comes running. "Boys! What are you doing?"

"He started it," I say.

When Mrs. Harper comes back to our room, Mr. Vogel talks to her for a while. She looks mad.

She tells Russell to move to Amanda's desk.

"I'm very disappointed in you boys," Mrs. Harper says.

She tells Amanda to move next to me.

I'm not disappointed.

September 19

We have band today. I have to sit next to Russell because we both play the trumpet. We have to share a music stand.

Russell still has not learned to be a good sharer.

He keeps pulling the music stand toward himself till I can't see the notes. I have to lean all the way over to read the music.

I lean farther and farther till our heads are practically touching. Suddenly he pulls his head away and blows a trumpet blast right in my ear.

"OW!" I hear *Clang! Clang!* in my ear. It hurts.

I reach under my chair and grab the carton of juice that I saved for lunch. I pour the juice into the bell of Russell's trumpet.

Russell jumps up and starts yelling and waving his trumpet around. Grape juice splatters on everyone in the brass section.

Mr. Strunk drops his baton and charges toward us. He looks angry. But I can't hear what he's saying because my ear is still clanging.

When I get home from school, my father asks me how my clothes got purple.

"It was Russell's fault," I tell him. "He splashed juice on everybody."

September 30
....

Mrs. Harper got mad at me again today.

But the goldfish didn't die.

And besides, it was Russell's fault.

October 4

You cannot trust Russell at dodgeball.

October 14

Tomorrow is Parent-Teacher Night. I am a little worried. I'm not sure Mrs. Harper will tell my father good things about me.

October 15

I am eating supper fast so we will get to Parent-Teacher Night on time. Mrs. Harper gets mad when you're late.

"Don't gulp your food, Bradley," my father says. "Proper chewing helps your fangs grow strong."

"I don't have fangs," I say.

"And you never will," he warns, "if you keep eating like that."

I pretend to eat slower.

"Isn't the lizard tender?" my father asks.

I nod. I push the fungus stir-fry around on my plate. I try to hide it under my lizard.

"Eat your fungus, Bradley," my father says. "It's very good for you. And I went to a lot of trouble to dig it up."

"You shouldn't go to so much trouble," I say.

A lot of cars are already in the parking lot when we get to school.

"I hope Mrs. Harper doesn't get mad at you," I say.

"Don't worry," my father says. "We're right on time."

A big sign over the door says, WELCOME, PARENTS!

We go inside, and I take my father down the hall to my classroom.

Mrs. Harper is standing by the classroom door. She is saying hello to Russell and his mother.

Russell sees me. He doesn't call me Stink-face. I don't call him Monkey Breath.

I take my father's hand. He smiles at Mrs.

Harper. "You must be Bradley's teacher," he says.

She looks at my father. She makes a funny noise. She moves her mouth, but no words come out.

Uh-oh. I start to think she might tell my father that I threw an eraser at Russell. Or that I hid his notebook in the fish tank. Or about dodgeball.

Russell's mother turns and sees us. She smiles.

"Well, hello there, Mr. Fentriss. How are you?"

"Fine, thank you, Mrs. Redfern. Has it really been a whole year since we've seen each other?"

"I guess it has been," she says. "Last Parent-Teacher Night, wasn't it?"

Mrs. Harper doesn't look so funny now. Maybe she won't tell my father bad things about me.

"So, you're Bradley's father," is all she says.

I show my father around the room.

He looks at the fish tank. He looks at the portraits on the wall.

"Where is your drawing?" he asks.

"Russell messed it up," I tell him.

"Why did he do that?" he asks.

"Russell is not a true art lover."

Everyone is looking at my father. He knows some of the parents and kids from last year. He smiles and says hello to everyone. Even to the parents he doesn't know.

"I want you to meet Amanda," I say. "She's my desk partner." I take his hand and pull him over to Amanda.

"This is Amanda," I tell him. "Amanda, this is my father."

Amanda looks up at my father. Way up. Her eyes get really big. She is probably surprised that he is so tall.

"Hello, Mr. Fentriss," she says.

"I'm glad to meet you, Amanda," my father says. "I saw your drawing on the wall. It's very good."

"Thank you." Amanda looks surprised. I'm

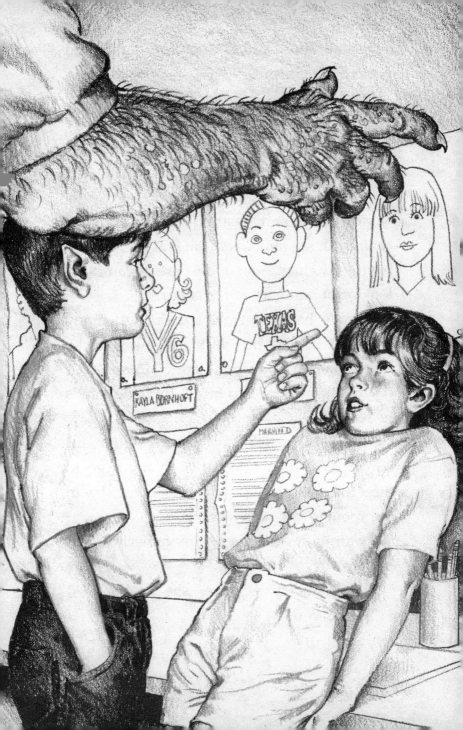

surprised, too. I didn't know my father had noticed her portrait.

"Parents," Mrs. Harper says loudly, "will you please sit down at your children's desks?"

"Amanda seems very nice," my father says as I take him to my desk.

"She is not a stinkface," I say.

Most of the parents are too big to fit in our chairs. But my father is so tall that he's *way* too big for my chair. A lot of the parents can't stop looking at him. I try not to laugh.

But it's hard. He really does look funny squished behind my desk. He takes up so much room that Amanda's father doesn't even try to sit down next to him. I think he thinks he won't fit.

Mrs. Harper tells our parents about our school day. Then some of the parents go to meet our special subject teachers. Some stay in our room to talk with Mrs. Harper.

I wait with Amanda for my father to come back to our room.

"Your father is very nice," she says.

"Thank you."

"Very tall," she says.

"I hope I grow that tall," I say.

Russell sneaks up behind me. "You will always be a dinky little shrimp," he says.

I whirl around. "You will always be a great big dope," I say.

My father comes back from meeting Mr. Vogel and Mr. Strunk. I hope Mr. Strunk didn't tell him that I poured grape juice into Russell's trumpet. I hope Mr. Vogel didn't tell him that I drew an X on Russell's nose.

My father and Mrs. Harper start talking.

I move up to the front of the room so I can hear what they are saying.

Mrs. Harper takes a deep breath. "I must tell you, Mr. Fentriss, that Bradley can sometimes be a perfect little monster."

My father's chest puffs out. It gets bigger and bigger. Two buttons pop off his shirt.

Mrs. Harper ducks under her desk. She is probably afraid she'll be hit by flying buttons.

My father smiles a big, proud smile. He is still smiling as he picks up his buttons from the floor.

Mrs. Harper peeks out from under her desk.

"Thank you so much, Mrs. Harper," he says. "That's very nice to hear."

She stands up. But she stays behind her desk.

"Mr. Fentriss," she says, "what I meant was—"

She stops. She looks at my my father.

Some of his hair is sticking out of his shirt. His fangs are gleaming. His eyes are bright and shiny.

"You're welcome," she says softly.

Holiday for Monsters

October 25

I can't wait for Halloween! It's my favorite holiday. My father always makes us costumes, and we go trick-or-treating together.

"What kind of a costume would you like this year?" my father asks.

"A scary one," I say.

"Do you want to be a vampire?"

"Vampires aren't scary," I say.

"A ghost?" he asks.

"Only babies wear ghost costumes," I say. "Nobody's scared of them."

"Hmm." He taps his claws against his chin. "I've got it! You can be a piranha."

"What's a piranha?"

"It's a fish," he says.

"A fish?" I say. "A fish isn't scary."

"A piranha is no ordinary fish," he says. "It's the most dangerous fish in the world. It has sharp, pointy teeth."

"Sharp teeth?" I say. "Like yours?"

"Sharper," he says. "Pointier." He pulls *The Big Book of Fish* from the bookcase. He opens it to a picture of a piranha.

"Wow!" I say. "That is an *ugly* fish!"

"You should not judge anyone by the way they look," my father reminds me. "But we might make an exception for piranhas."

"I want to be a piranha!"

"Then we'd better get started on your costume," my father says.

We go up to the attic. We open the old clothes trunk. My father pulls out a pair of gray pants. "These will be perfect for your fins," he says.

He finds a gray jacket that matches the pants. "We can use these for the rest of you."

"What about my teeth?" I ask. "How will we make my teeth?"

He thinks for a moment. "Popsicle sticks," he says.

"Popsicle sticks?" I am disappointed. "Popsicle sticks won't scare anybody."

"Yes, they will," he promises.

October 30

My father has been cutting and sewing for days.

I am beginning to worry that my costume won't be finished in time for Halloween.

"This is taking a long time," I tell him.

"It's a complicated costume," he says. "Especially the head."

When he isn't cutting and sewing, he is down in the basement. He says he is making my teeth. But he won't let me see them till he's done. "I want to surprise you," he says.

October 31 — Halloween

My costume is finished! Just in time!

"Come and put it on," my father says.

It's already six o'clock, and dark out.

We go into his bedroom. I step into my costume. It's all gray. There's a wide tail on the back that sticks out behind my feet. I slip my arms into the flippers, which are shaped like long triangles.

"Where's the rest of it?" I ask. "Where's my head? And my teeth?"

"Close your eyes," he says.

"Why?"

"You'll see."

I close my eyes. He slides something over my head. It feels like a hood, except it covers my whole face.

"Okay," he says. "You can open your eyes now."

I open my eyes. There's a narrow slit in the hood. I can see myself in the mirror on the closet door.

"Wow!"

My head is big and gray, with huge jaws. The mouth stays open, so you can see the rows of pointy white teeth attached to it.

I move closer to the mirror to look at my

teeth. "Cool!" I say. "No one could tell they're just Popsicle sticks."

"Watch this," my father says. He turns out the bedroom light. "Look at them now."

I look in the mirror. In the dim bedroom I can hardly see my gray costume. But I can see my teeth. They glow in the dark.

"*Awesome.*" I stare at my sharp, dazzling teeth.

"I used a special paint," my father says. "People will see your teeth coming before they see you."

"Yeah," I say happily. "But I wish they were real. I wish they were sharp enough to bite someone."

"Now, Bradley," my father says. "You don't really want to bite anyone, do you?"

"Only Russell," I say.

"I'll get my costume on," my father says. He opens his closet and disappears inside.

I hear him moving around. When he comes out, he is wearing a white shirt with puffy sleeves, and a wide red sash.

He has black pants and boots, and a black

patch over one eye. He's got a pirate hat with a skull-and-crossbones on it. There's even a parrot on his shoulder.

"Yo-ho-ho!" he roars. "What do you think?"

I stand on my toes to look at the parrot. "Is it real?" I ask. "Is it dead?"

"No. It's just a stuffed toy."

"Oh."

"Well," he says, "do you like my costume?"

"It's very nice," I say. "But you're not too scary."

"You're scary enough for both of us," he says.

"But everyone around here knows you," I say. "So they won't be scared of me when they see you with me."

"Hmm." He thinks for a minute. "I know!" he says. "We'll go someplace that we've never been to before. We'll go trick-or-treating where no one knows us."

"Yes!" I clap my flippers. "That's a good idea. Let's go really far away."

"Well, not too far," he says. "Tomorrow is a school day."

I get my big plastic pumpkin to hold my treats. We go out to the car. Kids are running up and down our street. They ring doorbells and shriek and giggle.

No one else has a piranha costume. No one else has teeth that glow in the dark.

I get into the car. My father helps me tuck my tail in.

We start driving to Canterville, which is about twenty mintues away from our house. I can't wait to start scaring people, but my father is driving very slowly.

"Come on!" I say. "Go faster! We'll never get there."

"Safety first," he says. "It would be danger-ous to drive fast with so many children out tonight."

We finally get to Canterville. We park the car on a block with a lot of big houses. There are hardly any children around.

"I'll bet they have lots of candy still left!" I say excitedly.

We get out of the car and walk up to the

door of the corner house. My father stands a little behind me as I ring the bell.

A woman with red hair opens the door.

"Trick or treat!" I say.

She screams. She slams the door.

"Hey, wait!" I yell. "Where's my treat?"

I see the top of the woman's head and her eyes, peeking through a front window.

"Wow," I say. "I must have really scared her."

"Well, that's what you wanted to do," my father says.

"Yes, but I want my treats, too."

"Let's try the next house," my father says. "Maybe you won't scare them so badly."

We walk to the next house. I ring the doorbell. "Trick or treat!" I call.

The door opens. A short old lady with curly gray hair looks out at us. Her eyes grow big. Her mouth drops open.

"Oh, my," she says. She looks very scared.

"Trick or treat!" I say again. "And I'm not a real piranha. This is just my costume."

She still looks scared. It must be my glow-in-the-dark teeth.

"And he's not a real pirate." I point a fin at my father. But she is already staring at him. She stands as still as a statue in the doorway.

"May I please have a treat?" I ask politely. I am beginning to worry that my costume is so scary that no one will give me any candy.

The lady doesn't take her eyes off us. But she reaches behind herself for something. Still staring at us, she holds out a big bowl of miniature chocolates.

"Yippee!" I scoop a flipperful of candy from the bowl.

"Bradley," my father says, "don't be greedy. Leave some candy for the other children."

The woman looks at my father nervously.

I drop most of the candy back in the bowl. I keep only two pieces. I put them in my plastic pumpkin.

"Thank you," I say.

"And Happy Halloween," my father says. The woman just blinks a few times. Then she carefully closes the door. I can hear a *thunk* as the lock turns.

"Wow!" I yell. "I *really* scared her!" I run to the next house.

I ring the doorbell. A teenage boy opens the door. He is wearing headphones. He hardly even looks at us. He just tosses a couple of candy-corn packets into my pumpkin.

I am disappointed that he isn't frightened of me.

"You know what they say, Bradley," my father reminds me. "You can't scare all of the people all of the time."

But I do scare most of the people. One man even dumps his whole bag of candy into my pumpkin before he jumps back inside his house and slams the door.

"Wow." We turn the corner to start up the next block. "There sure are a lot of nervous people around here."

We go from house to house, scaring almost everybody.

Finally my father, says, "Time to go home."

I don't even argue, because my pumpkin is practically bursting with treats. It's so full, I couldn't stuff one more piece of candy corn into it.

"This is the best trick-or-treating we ever did!" I say. We get into our car. "I never scared so many people in my whole life."

"You looked very frightening," my father agrees.

"Yeah," I say happily.

He checks my seat belt. Then he starts the car. He makes a U-turn and heads for home.

I give him a lollipop. "I love Halloween," I say.

I hear a loud crunch as he bites through the hard part of the pop to the chocolate in the middle.

"I know you do," he says.

Then I think maybe he's disappointed because I was more frightening than he was. I think maybe I shouldn't have told him his pirate costume wasn't scary.

"They might have been a little afraid of

you, too," I say. "I guess *some* people are scared of pirates."

"It's all right, Bradley," my father says. "Scaring people is probably more fun for you than it is for me."

Monster in
the Attic

December 3

We are watching "Jeopardy!" My father
is shouting out all the answers.

"What are death cap mushrooms?"

"Who is Martha Stewart?"

"What is Devil's Island?"

"You never give me a chance to answer," I
complain.

"I'm sorry," my father says. "I just get so excited." He looks down at his pad. "I've already
won seven thousand dollars. And I didn't get
one question wrong."

I look down at my pad. I have won no dollars. And I haven't gotten one question *right*.

"You know you're going to come in first," I
say. "You always come in first."

"But you can never tell about Final Jeopardy," he says. "It might be a really hard category. Like 'Fine China.' Or 'Horror Movies.' "

Just as the Final Jeopardy category is announced, we hear a weird cracking sound over our heads.

"What's that?" I ask.

"I don't know," my father says.

Now there's a groaning, crunching noise, and then something that sounds like a shower of rocks hitting the roof.

"Earthquake!" I scream.

"We don't get earthquakes here," my father says. He puts down his pad. "But *something* is quaking."

We go upstairs. We look in his bedroom. Everything is fine. We look into the bathroom. The bathroom is fine. We look in my room.

"Good heavens!" my father cries.

There's a crack in the ceiling of my room. Pieces of plaster and paint chips are scattered over my bed.

The ceiling creaks and groans again. Even as we look at it, the crack grows longer.

"How did that happen?" I ask.

"We'd better go check."

We climb upstairs to the attic. The attic has a regular floor down the middle. On the sides there are big spaces with long narrow wood boards between them. The spaces are filled with fluffy gray stuff.

We see right away what the problem is. Somehow the old clothes trunk has slid partway off the floor and into the gray stuff.

"The earthquake must have made the trunk slip," I say.

"There was no earthquake," my father says. "But I'd better pull the trunk back before it falls through the insulation."

He tugs at the trunk, trying to pull it back onto the floor. But it's hard to get hold of. He can't grip it, and his claws make scratches along the sides of the trunk. It starts slipping even more.

I hear another crack and some clattering sounds. I know more ceiling must be falling into my room.

"I'll have to push it up instead of pulling it,"

my father says. He walks carefully onto one of the beams, like he's balancing on a tightrope. He leans down and tries to push the trunk from underneath.

Suddenly his hand slips, and he starts to topple over. He grabs for the beam but misses. His sharp claws slash right through the insulation. He slides off the beam and tumbles out of sight.

"Yikes!" Just in time he grabs onto the beam and sinks his claws into it. Now I can see his hands and his claws and the very top of his head.

"Dad!"

"Don't worry, Bradley." His voice is muffled. He makes coughing and spitting sounds. "Everything's under control."

"I'll help you! I'll pull you up."

"No, don't try that." He sneezes. "Go down to your room and put a chair under me."

I run downstairs to my room. My bed is covered with huge chunks of ceiling. The bottom part of my father is dangling from the attic like a piñata.

I slide my desk chair under his feet. "Okay! You can let go now."

He lets go. He drops through the ceiling and lands on the chair.

He is covered with gray stuff. He sneezes and coughs and tries to scrape the insulation off his tongue. He shakes his head and rubs at his eyes.

"Are you okay?" I ask nervously. "Is anything broken?"

"Only the ceiling," he says.

We look up at my ceiling. Now there isn't just a crack in it. There's a big hole where my father fell. And one corner of the trunk is sticking through the hole, right over my bed.

"Wow!" I say. "Good thing I wasn't sleeping."

"Oh, dear." My father puts his hand on his heart. "That trunk could have fallen right on top of you."

"You would have fallen on top of me first," I say. "Then the trunk."

He closes his eyes. He sneezes again. "Let's not talk about it," he says.

"What do we do now?" I ask.

"We'd better call Ms. Wainsocket," he says. "She can fix anything."

We go back to the living room. My father looks up Wendy Wainsocket's We-Fix-Anything in our address book. He dials her number.

He hangs up the phone. "She won't be in till Monday," he says. "I only got her answering machine."

"Maybe we can fix it ourselves," I say.

"I don't know about that," my father says.

"We painted the kitchen," I say. "And we built my bookshelves."

"That's true," he says. "Though the shelves turned out a little bit slanty."

"They do sort of tilt," I say, "but they hold my books."

"You're right, Bradley," my father says. "You never know what you can do until you try."

He gets out *The Big Book of Home Repair* and starts looking through the index. " 'Ceilings,' " he mutters. " 'Ceiling bulges, ceiling cracks, ceiling decoration.' Here we go: 'Ceilings falling down.' "

He pages through the chapter on ceilings falling down.

"This doesn't look too hard," he says.

"Before we fix it," I say, "can I jump through the hole?"

"No," he says. "That would not be a good idea."

He starts to list the things we'll need to fix the ceiling. "Plaster, gypsum, lumber, furring strips—"

"Furry strips?" I ask.

"No. Furring strips."

"What are they?"

He sighs. "I don't know."

We go down to the basement to see if we have any of the stuff we need to fix my ceiling.

We have plaster. We have some boards left over from building my bookshelves. We have painter's caps from when we painted the kitchen.

We don't have any gypsum. I don't know

what gypsum is, but my father says we don't have any.

Leaning up against the basement wall is an old Ping-Pong table. "The perfect thing!" my father says. "We can cut it to fit the hole, then plaster over it."

We put on our painter's caps. My father picks up the Ping-Pong table and holds it under his arm. He pulls a bunch of nails from a jar and sticks them into his mouth, one between each of his fangs.

"Let me hold the nails!" I say. "I want to hold the nails in my teeth."

"Your teeth aren't big enough yet," he says, talking right through the nails. "And they're too close together. I don't want you holding nails in your mouth till your fangs grow in."

"My fangs will never grow in," I say.

"Why don't you help me by carrying the hammer and the tape measure?" he says.

"Okay. But I'd rather hold nails in my mouth."

We carry the Ping-Pong table and the nails and hammer and tape measure up to the attic.

"We still have to pull the trunk out of my ceiling," I say.

"Now it will be easy," my father says. He lays the Ping-Pong table across the beams and the insulation. He stands on the table and pushes the trunk back easily onto the attic floor.

"I wish I'd thought of this before," he says. He sneezes and tries to brush insulation out of his hair.

He goes back to the basement. I pick up some nails and try to hold them between my teeth. The nails are yucky tasting, cold and hard. I spit them out into my hand.

I look through the hole into my room. I really want to jump through it.

My father comes back to the attic with a power saw, an electric drill, and a Dustbuster. He pulls sandpaper and a stick of chalk from his pockets.

"Are we going to need all that?" I ask.

"I'm not sure," he says. "But it's best to be prepared before you start a project."

I pick up the Dustbuster. "Do you want me to vacuum you?"

"After we fix the ceiling," he says. "It might be a messy job."

"It's already a messy job," I tell him.

He measures the hole in the attic floor with the tape measure. He makes a chalk outline on the Ping-Pong table in the shape of the hole.

"Now we'll cut the table to fit and hammer it down," he says.

"Before you close up the hole," I say, "could I jump down to my bed just once?"

"No, Bradley," he says firmly. "Jumping through ceilings is dangerous."

He picks up the saw and looks around for a place to plug it in. There is an outlet next to the lightbulb hanging from the rafters.

He plugs in the saw. "Here we go," he says. He turns on the saw.

It whirs loudly. He begins to cut through the edge of the Ping-Pong table.

The lightbulb goes out. The saw stops whirring. The attic is completely dark. My room is dark. I don't hear the television anymore.

"What happened?" I ask.

"I think I must have tripped a circuit breaker," my father says.

"What does that mean?"

"It means I have to go to the basement and see if I can turn the electricity back on," he says.

"It's so dark, I can't see a thing," I tell him.

"We'll have to be very careful on the stairs," my father says. "Follow me. I'll help you down."

"You don't have to," I say. "There's an easier way. *Geronimo!*" I yell, and jump through the hole in the attic floor.

I make a perfect landing on my bed. I bounce once and come down again. The legs of my bed collapse with a loud crash.

"Uh-oh," I say.

"Bradley!" my father cries. "What happened?"

"That was cool!" I call up to him. "I'm going to it again."

He sticks his head down through the hole in the ceiling. "I told you not to jump," he scolds. "Are you all right? Is anything broken?"

"Only my bed."

I hear him thump down the attic stairs. He comes into my room.

"Does *The Big Book of Home Repair* tell you how to fix broken beds?" I ask.

"I don't know," he says. "But without the lights on, I can hardly see the bed."

"You know what?" I say. "If there was a hole in my floor, we could jump right down to the living room. And then if there was a hole in the living room floor, we could jump right down to the basement."

"I'm having enough trouble fixing one hole," my father says. "I would not care to fix three holes."

"And a bed," I remind him.

"And a bed," he says. "Now I want you to stay here and *not move* while I go check the circuit breakers."

"Okay," I say.

"Don't bounce on anything. Don't jump

through anything. Just stand right where you are and tell me when the lights come back on."

"Okay."

I wait right where I am while my father goes down to the basement.

"Are the lights on yet?" he calls.

"No!"

Another minute. Then he yells, "Are they on yet?"

"Not yet!" I answer.

I hear him walking up the stairs again. He comes into my room with a flashlight.

"What's the matter?" I ask. "How come the lights didn't come back on?"

He doesn't answer me right away. He shines the flashlight around my room. We can see the bed. Three of the legs are broken. The mattress has slipped off onto the floor.

There are pieces of ceiling all over the bed. There are pieces of ceiling all over my room.

"Wow," I say. "What a mess. We have a lot of fixing do."

"Bradley," my father says slowly, "I have an idea. Why don't we sleep at the Happy Wanderer Motel tonight? They have in-room movies and beds that give you a massage."

"Yay!" I yell. "Can I get room service?"

"I don't know if they have room service," my father says.

"But when will we fix the ceiling?" I ask. "And my bed? And the lights?"

He puts his arm around my shoulder and leads me into the hall. He shines the flashlight on the stairs so we can see our way down.

"It's important to know your limits," he says. "Some jobs should be left to experts."

"Does that mean we're not going to fix the ceiling?" I ask.

"I'll call Ms. Wainsocket in the morning and ask her to do it. Even though it's the weekend."

"What about my bed?"

"That, too," my father says.

"And the electricity?"

"Especially the electricity," my father says. "Electric repairs should always be done by a trained expert."

"Then we're not going to fix *anything*?" I'm kind of disappointed.

"No," my father says. "But we'll have a fine time at the motel."

"Yeah!" I get excited again. "I'm going to order shrimp cocktail from room service. And hot wings. And I'm going to watch a movie and have the bed massage me."

We get our jackets out of the front closet. I still have my painter's cap on.

"And when Ms. Wainsocket comes," I say, "maybe we can help her with the repairs."

My father takes the painter's cap off my head. He takes his painter's cap off. He puts both of them on the closet shelf.

"I think we'd better not," he says.

Sunday in the Park with Monsters

December 13

When I wake up this morning, it is snowing.

I run to the window. Everything is white. The trees, the yard, the street. I can't see the sidewalk. There's a pile of snow on the birdbath.

"Yay!"

I run into my father's room. "It's snowing! It's snowing!"

I jump onto the bed and land on his stomach.

"Ooff," he grunts. "You're getting big, Bradley."

"Are my teeth big yet?" I spread my lips so he can see.

"Not yet. Be patient." He looks over to

the window. "It *is* snowing." He sounds surprised.

"I know! I told you!" I tug the covers off him. "Where's my sled? Where are my boots? Can we make snow cones?"

"Breakfast first," he says. "A healthy breakfast is the start of a healthy day."

We go down to the kitchen, and my father prepares his coffee. "Would you like waffles today?" he asks.

I love waffles. But today I am not interested in anything but snow.

"I want to go sledding!" I say. "I want to make snow cones! I want to build a snow person!"

My father looks out the kitchen window. He gets a funny, dreamy look in his eyes.

"I feel like a picnic," he says.

"A picnic? But it's snowing. You can't have a picnic in the snow."

He pours himself a cup of coffee. "Why not?"

"Because it's too cold."

"We will dress warmly," he says.

"There's no grass to sit on," I say.

"There's grass," he says. "Under the snow."

"But it's *winter!*"

"Yes, it is." He gets that faraway look in his eyes again. "And when you were very little, we had a picnic in the snow."

"We did?"

He nods. "It was your mother's idea. It was the best picnic we ever had."

"Mom must have been fun," I say.

"She was." He picks me up and plops me onto a chair. "And so are you," he says.

He cooks me some oatmeal and starts making sandwiches.

"We'll have all your favorites," he says. "Peanut butter and jellyfish. Deviled squid. And a nice big jug of cream of fungus soup to keep us warm."

"Can I take my sled?" I ask.

"Of course."

"Can we make snow cones?" I ask.

"I'll pack the syrup in the picnic basket," he says.

"Do I have to eat the cream of fungus soup?"

"We'll bring some hot chocolate, too."

After breakfast we start collecting all the things we will need for our picnic.

My father packs the basket full of food. He helps me on with my boots. We find my snow-ball gloves, the ones with the leather palms, so the snow doesn't soak through.

I put on my gloves. He puts on a pair of snowshoes. He wraps a scarf around my neck. We both put on our wool caps. Mine is blue with white snowflake designs on it. His is a red stocking cap with a white pom-pom on the end.

It's still snowing. When we go outside, the walk is so icy that I fall down the minute I step off the porch. But I don't hurt myself. I'm so bundled up, I can hardly feel anything.

"Don't forget my sled," I say.

"We can't forget your sled," he says. "It's too slippery to drive."

He opens the garage and gets my sled out. He sets it down on the sidewalk. I sit down on the sled. "Let's go!"

"Just a minute." He goes back into the

garage. He gets the fold-up tent and a blanket. He puts the blanket on my lap. He puts the tent on top of the blanket. He sets the picnic basket on top of the tent.

"Can you hold on to all that?" he asks.

"Sure. Let's go!"

He starts to close the garage door.

"Oops. Nearly forgot something," he says.

He goes back into the garage.

When he comes out, he is carrying a big yellow kite. He places it on the pile already on my lap.

"We're going to fly a kite?" I ask. "In the *snow?*"

"It's a plastic kite," he says. "The snow won't hurt it."

I have so much stuff loaded on my lap that I don't even see when he picks up the rope on the sled. But all of a sudden I feel myself skimming down the icy street.

"Whee!"

The ride to the park is great. I keep tilting over and falling off the sled and falling into the snow. My father has to keep stacking all the picnic stuff, and me, back onto the sled.

At the park my father pulls the sled under a big tree. There are no leaves on the branches. But they're covered with ice and they look all silvery.

"This is a good spot for a picnic," he says.

He unloads all the picnic stuff, and me, from the sled.

"First we'll put up our tent," he says.

He unfolds the tent. A big gust of wind flaps it up and down as he's holding it. Then the wind whips sideways. The tent twirls around my father till it wraps him up like a mummy.

"Wmmff!" he says from inside the tent.

I think he is probably asking me to help. So I tug at one end of the tent and start to unwind it.

"Maybe it's too windy to put up a tent," I say after I unwrap my father.

"It's too windy *not* to put up a tent," he says.

He reaches into his pocket. "Luckily I remembered to bring the tent pegs."

He takes one of the pegs and tries to push it into the ground. He pushes and pushes, but it won't go in.

"I guess the ground is frozen," I say.

He nods. "Unluckily I forgot to bring a hammer."

He scratches around in the snow till he finds a large rock. "We'll use this for a hammer."

I look across the park. A few kids are sledding down a little hill on the other side.

"Can I go sledding?" I ask.

My father is grunting and panting and pounding the pegs into the hard dirt. I can see his chest puffing up, even under his heavy jacket. "As soon as we get the tent up," he says.

I help by holding on to one edge of the tent while he fastens the other ends to the pegs. It isn't easy because the wind keeps blowing and it's hard to hold on. Sometimes the wind grabs the tent right out of my hands. Sometimes I think if that I don't let go, the wind will pick up the tent and me and blow me across the park.

But at last the tent is up.

"Yay! Now can I go sledding?"

"Yes," my father says. "You go sledding while I get our picnic ready." He is already spreading out the blanket inside the tent.

"Be careful!" he calls as I start toward the hill. "Watch out for other sledders! No crashing!"

"Okay!"

I pull my sled across the park to the little hill. There are three small kids hanging on to their parents. And Amanda is there. She's wearing a red parka with a hood.

"Hi, Amanda!"

"Hi, Bradley."

"We're having a picnic," I tell her.

"A picnic?" she says. "Cool."

"We have a tent and everything," I say. "Want to come?"

"Sure," she says. "If it's okay with your father."

"He won't mind," I say. "He made tons of food."

I throw myself on my sled, facedown. *"Geronimo!"* I yell, and the sled takes off, coasting down the slope. Snowflakes smack my cheeks, and the wind blows snow in my eyes. I can hardly see the bottom of the hill till I get there.

It is great.

I roll off the sled just as Amanda comes flying down the hill on her sled.

"Pocahontas!" she yells, and nearly crashes into me at the bottom.

We pull our sleds up the hill and go down again, this time side by side.

The third time we start back up the hill, I see my father at the top.

"The picnic must be ready," I tell Amanda.

The little kids on the hill are all staring at my father. One of them runs to her mother and grabs her coat. She peeks out from behind it.

I start to laugh. "See his hat?" I say to Amanda. "I'll bet they think he's Santa Claus."

"He does look sort of like Santa Claus,"

Amanda says. "Except for his hair." She waves. "Hi, Mr. Fentriss!"

"Hello, Amanda," he says as we pull our sleds up next to him. "The sledding looks excellent today."

"It is," Amanda says. "You should try it."

"Oh, no," my father says, patting her gently on her hood. "I haven't been sledding for years. I'm not sure I remember how."

"It's not hard." Amanda takes his hand and pulls him toward her sled. "And it's fun."

"Well . . ." He takes a deep breath. He looks around.

No one else is sledding now. The kids and parents are all bunched together in a little group. They're staring at him. I think maybe he feels embarrassed to try sledding with everyone watching.

"Let's all go together," I say.

"Good idea!" Amanda says. "Come on, Mr. Fentriss."

"Well . . ."

But he climbs onto Amanda's sled. He sits on the end. I sit between his legs, and Amanda sits in front of me. We push our hands against the ground to get started.

Then, *whoosh!* We're zooming down the hill, yelling, *"Geronimo!"* and *"Pocahontas!"* and *"Look out below!"*

We hit a bump at the bottom, and we all go sprawling off into the snow.

Amanda is laughing, and I am laughing. My father is rolling around in the snow like a little kid, making whooping noises.

"Wasn't that fun?" Amanda says. She holds out her hand to help him up.

"Yes!" my father says. "Yes! Let's go again!"

By the time we pull the sled back up the hill, my father's chest has gotten so big that I'm glad his jacket has a zipper. It would be very hard to find buttons in the snow.

We go zooming down all together one more time. Then my father decides he wants to try sledding on his own.

He does a belly flop onto my sled and slides down the hill. At the bottom, he jumps off the sled, then pulls it back to the top and goes down again. And again. Sometimes he

goes headfirst, and sometimes he sleds with his knees up, waving one arm like a rodeo cowboy.

He's laughing and hollering, and soon the other kids are riding their sleds down the hill beside him. Their parents are laughing, too, seeing how much fun everyone is having.

Amanda and I have to double up on her sled, because my father won't let go of mine.

I don't mind. Sledding with Amanda is okay. Even if we fall off a lot.

But I am starting to get hungry. I'm starting to think that my father is having so much fun that he's forgotten about our picnic.

At last he brushes and shakes the snow off himself and says, "That was a fine morning's sledding! Now I think we should eat our picnic lunch."

"Yay!" I say. "I'm starving."

"Won't you join us, Amanda?" he asks.

"I'd like that," she says. "Sledding makes me hungry."

"Me, too."

My father waves good-bye to the other sledders, and we walk across the park to our tent. We go inside. There's a red-and-white-checked tablecloth spread over the blanket.

"Sit down, sit down," he tells us.

He starts to fill plastic plates with sandwiches and deviled squid and hard-boiled eggs. He opens the jugs of cream of fungus soup and hot chocolate.

He hands around napkins and plastic forks.

He pulls a Bug-Off candle from the picnic basket and puts it in the center of the tablecloth.

"What do we need that for?" I ask.

He lights the candle. "To keep the bugs away," he says.

"But there aren't any bugs," I say.

"You see?" he says. "It's working."

We eat sandwiches and drink hot chocolate. Amanda says, "No, thank you," to the soup and the squid. But she drinks two cups of cocoa and eats two sandwiches. The wind howls around the tent, pushing the sides in. But the tent stays up.

Every once in a while, someone comes and

looks inside to see what we're doing. A few of the sledders and parents peek in, and my father invites them to share our picnic.

Even the little girl who hid behind her mother sits down with us and eats two cookies.

All of a sudden I see Russell's head poking through the tent.

"Hey, it's Stinkface!" he says.

"Go away," I say. "This is our picnic, and you're not invited."

"Bradley," my father says, "remember your manners."

"I remember them," I say, "I just don't want to use them."

"Would you like some cream of fungus soup?" my father asks Russell. "How about some nice deviled squid?"

"Yuck!" Russell yells. He pulls his head back, and we hear him tromp away through the snow.

"Too bad he couldn't stay," my father says. "And just when we were going to make snow cones."

He pulls a stack of little paper cups out of the picnic basket. He gives me one and Amanda one, and the three little kids and their parents each get one, too.

We all go outside and start scooping clean snow into our cups.

One father says, "What's a snow cone?" Even though he doesn't know what it is, he scoops up a cupful of snow.

My father comes out of the tent with the bottle of vanilla syrup. Everybody rushes toward him, holding up their cups. Even the man who doesn't know how to make a snow cone.

My father pours syrup into everybody's cup. All the kids stick their faces into their cups and start slurping down the sweet, cold snow.

He slides his own soup mug through a big drift till he has a huge portion of snow in it. He pours a ton of vanilla syrup on it. He sucks the top and smiles. "Delicious," he says. "You see, Bradley? We couldn't make snow cones at an ordinary picnic."

At last, all the syrup is used up. All the food is used up, too. Except for some cream of fungus soup. Everyone starts saying, "Goodbye!" and "Thank you!" and "Great picnic!"

Even Amanda has to leave. "I told my mother I'd be home for lunch," she says. She pats her stomach. "I don't think I'm going to eat much lunch."

I am sorry she is going. She is really a very good sledder.

"I had a wonderful time, Mr. Fentriss." She picks up her sled. "This was an excellent picnic."

When she is gone, we clean up all the paper plates and forks and napkins. We put everything in a plastic trash bag.

"Bradley, find a garbage can and throw this out," my father says. "Then we'll fly our kite."

I drag the bag to a big metal can near a water fountain.

I come back, and my father is unwinding the kite string.

"You know what?" I say.

"What?"

"I think this is the best idea you ever had."

He smiles. His smile gets bigger and bigger. His chest gets bigger and bigger.

"I think so, too," he says.

He lets out the kite string and starts running. I run after him. The wind picks up the kite and snaps it into the air.

We race across the park, through the snowflakes, into the wind, until our kite is sailing toward the sky.